The Zebra who was Sad

Designer: Fiona Hajée

Consultant: Cecilia A. Essau, Professor of Developmental
Psychopathology at Roehampton University

Copyright © QED Publishing 2012

First published in the UK in 2012 by
QED Publishing
A Quarto Group Company
230 City Road
London EC1V 2TT

www.qed-publishing.co.uk

A catalogue record for this book is available from
the British Library.

ISBN 978 1 84835 849 2

Printed in China

The Zebra who was Sad

Rachel Elliot
John Bendall-Brunello

QED Publishing

Zebra was feeling very, very sad.
His best friend Giraffe was moving to the
other side of the jungle. They wouldn't be
able to play together any more.

"I'll miss you so much,"
said Zebra.

"I'll miss you too,"
said Giraffe.
"I promise to
write to you."

But Zebra didn't want letters.
He wanted his best friend to stay nearby.

When Giraffe left, Zebra cried and cried.

"Cheer up," said his dad.
"You can still visit Giraffe."

"But what if Giraffe makes new
friends and doesn't want me to be
her best friend any more?"

Zebra couldn't feel happy at all.

The other animals
wanted to stop Zebra
feeling sad. They tried
to cheer him up.

"Come and play chase with us!"
said Cheetah Cub.

Zebra joined
the game.

He tried to
have fun...

...but he kept
thinking about his
best friend.

"Giraffe loves
playing chase," he said.
"I wish she was here."

"Come and play catch," said Little Monkey.

They played with bunches of berries.

Zebra caught some berries on his back. Everyone cheered and shouted his name.

Zebra felt a little bit better.

After the game, they shared the berries.
They were ripe and juicy.

"Giraffe loves berries,"
said Zebra.

He felt sad that he had been
having fun without her.

"Let's play hide and seek,"
said Snake.

It was Zebra's turn to seek.
He looked everywhere
for his friends.

Little Elephant was easy to find.

"Found you!"

Hippo hid in the muddy river.
He pretended to be a log floating on the water,
but then Zebra saw him blink.

"Found you!"

Snake thought of a really clever place to hide.
It took Zebra ages to find him!

Then Zebra noticed
that the tree trunk looked
bigger than normal.

"Found you!"

When everyone had been found,
Little Monkey told some jokes.

He knew some really funny ones.

Zebra laughed so hard
that his ribs hurt!

Just then, Zebra's dad
came to find him.

"There's a letter for you,"
he said with a big smile.
"Can you guess who it's from?"

The letter was
written on a big leaf.

Dear Zebra,

We have arrived in our
new home. It's nice, but
I miss you and all our friends.

There is a friendly meerkat
here who is going to
show me around.

Please write soon.

Love from Giraffe
x x x

Zebra looked around at all his friends.

"I've got lots to tell Giraffe,"
he said. "She sounds sad
but Monkey's jokes will
make her laugh!"

"Your letter will
cheer her up,"
said his dad.

"That's what friends are for,"
said Zebra, smiling.
"Friends make you feel happy!"

Next steps

- Look at the front cover of the book together. Ask your child to name all the animals in the book: zebra, hippo, giraffe, monkey, cheetah, snake and elephant.

- Discuss the shape and colour of each animal and find out together where they live and what they eat.

- Ask your child which animal they like the most and why. If they could have one animal as a pet, which animal would they like to have?

- Ask your child what made Zebra feel sad. Then discuss how they knew Zebra felt sad.

- Ask your child if they remember what Zebra said and did when he was sad.

From sad to happy...

- Ask your child what eventually made Zebra feel happy.

- At the end of the story, ask your child to name one activity or thing that makes them feel happy, and another activity or thing that makes them feel sad.

- Ask your child to draw one picture of them feeling sad, and another picture of them feeling happy. Discuss what thoughts make your child sad or happy, as well as how they look when they are happy or sad (focus on their posture and facial expression).

- Emphasize to your child that there are ways to cheer themselves up when they are feeling sad. They could try some fun activities with their friends. Sharing their feelings with their friends may also help them feel better. They should also try and avoid any negative thoughts.